To kids everywhere—never be afraid to rep where you
come from. Whether it's the suburbs, a small town, or
the hood, remember that YOU are what makes it good. —DR

For Miranda —GJ

About This Book

The illustrations for this book were illustrated digitally in Adobe Fresco and Photoshop. This book was edited by Samantha Gentry and designed by Jenny Kimura. The production was supervised by Kimberly Stella, and the production editor was Annie McDonnell. The text was set in Excelcior LT Std, and the display type was hand lettered by the artist.

ALL GOOD IN THE HOOD

By DWAYNE REED

Illustrated by GLADYS JOSE

LB
LITTLE, BROWN AND COMPANY
New York Boston

Today is June 19th, Juneteenth's what they say.
And for Black people, it's a very special day.
"We're going to the park," Mom said. "It's a holiday!"
But, deep down, at home is where I wished we could stay.

"C'mon, let's celebrate!" I heard Dad say.

"There's music and food and games you can play."

But what would it be like? 'Cuz here, I'm safe and sound.

The hood feels scary when we're walking around.

My Big Bro could tell I was feelin' kinda worried,
So he gave me a smile, and a hug, in a hurry.
He calmed me down, like only big brothers could,
And said, "Don't worry, Lil' Bro, it's all good in the hood!"

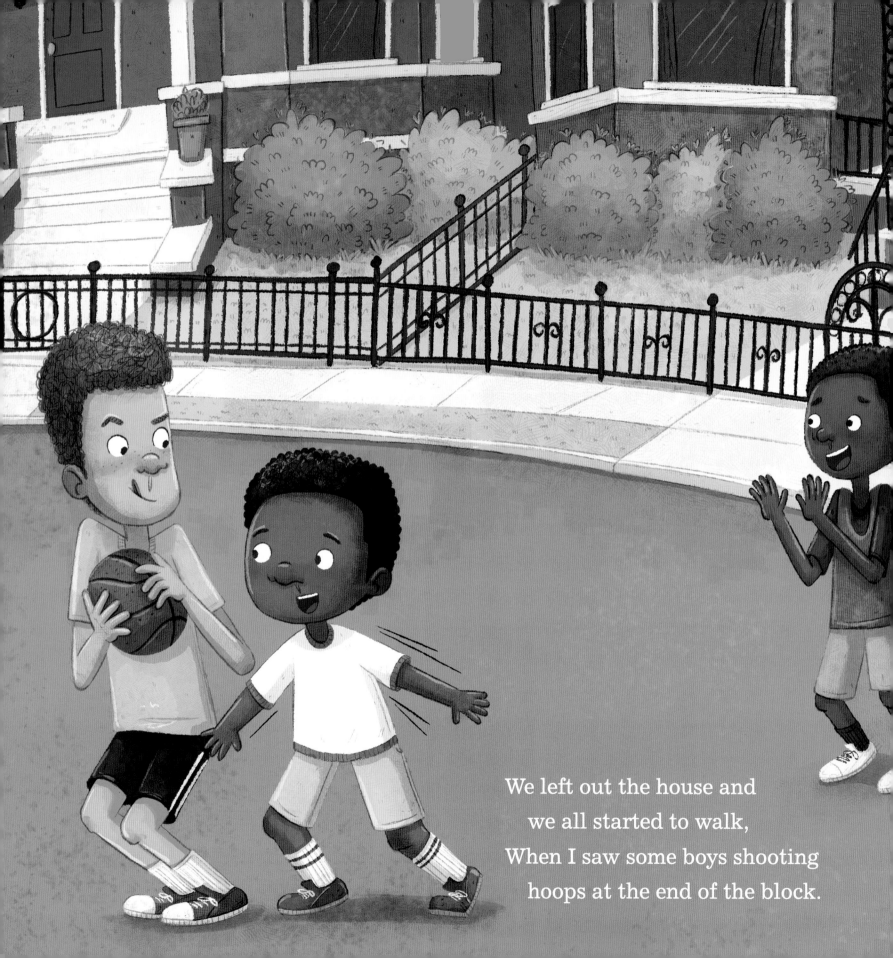

We left out the house and
we all started to walk,
When I saw some boys shooting
hoops at the end of the block.

I said, "Hey, I wanna play!" And the boys
    just laughed.
But Big Bro said, "C'mon, y'all, give him a pass."

But the pass was too fast, so the ball went out of reach,
And it tipped off my hands, then landed in the street.
When I ran to go grab it, Dad YELLED, Mom SHRIEKED!

Then out of nowhere, all we heard was

BEEP! BEEP!

It was the sound of a truck speeding fast.

As it *ZOOMED* toward me, I just knew it could crash.

But my Big Bro grabbed me
and pulled me to the side

Just in the nick of time as the
truck flew by.

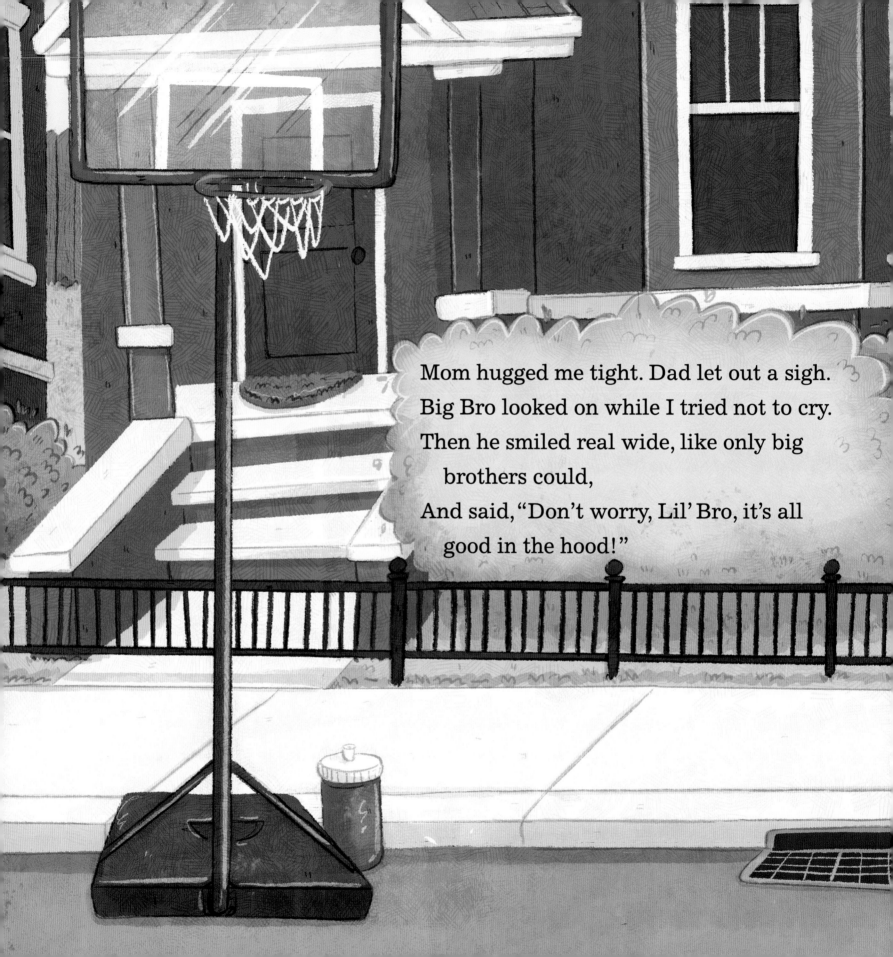

Mom hugged me tight. Dad let out a sigh.
Big Bro looked on while I tried not to cry.
Then he smiled real wide, like only big
    brothers could,
And said, "Don't worry, Lil' Bro, it's all
    good in the hood!"

A little bit later, we were almost to the park,
When I heard a loud

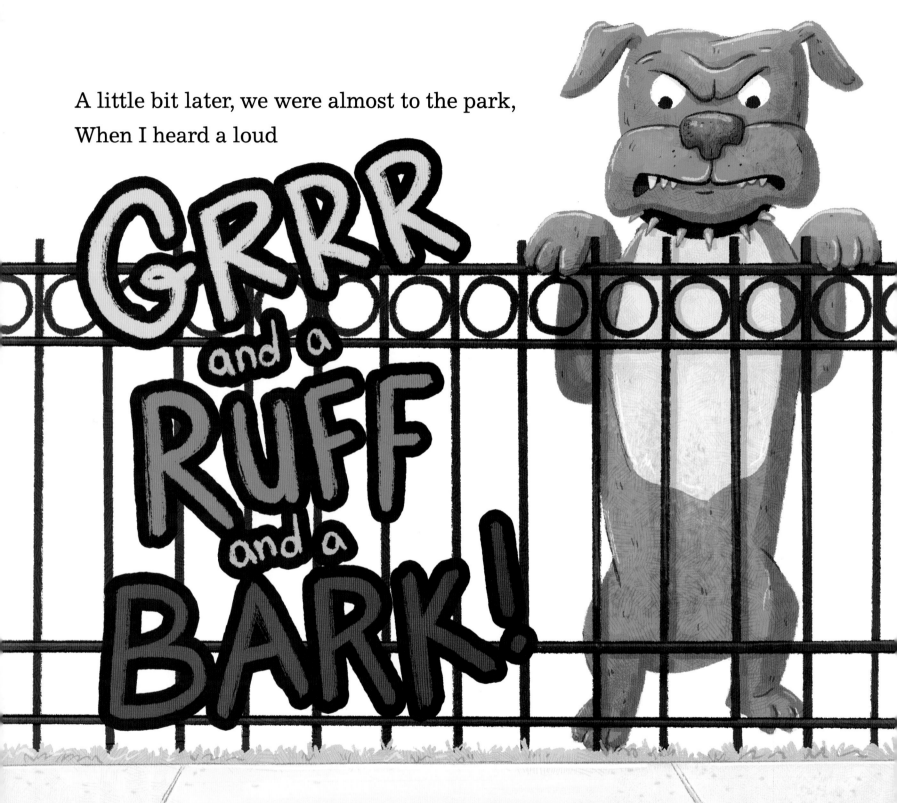

GRRR
and a
RUFF
and a
BARK!

A big, scary dog stood there behind a gate,
And its sharp yellow teeth made me begin to shake!

I screamed out, "Ma! That dog's gonna bite!"
Then I grabbed on her leg, and I held really tight.

Dad said, "You're all right! Big Bro will keep you safe!"
Then my brother jumped up and he rushed to the gate.
He yelled at the dog, and he told it to

"SCRAM!"

And the dog jumped back,
   then it **SQUEALED**, and it ran.

Bro made the dog leave, like only big brothers could,
And said, "Don't worry, Lil' Bro, it's all good in the hood!"

We were finally at the park, and Dad said, "What a crowd!"
There were so many people, and the voices were loud.
There were grannies chit-chattin' on seats in the shade.
"SNOW CONES!" yelled a man. **"ICE-COLD LEMONADE!"**

"I don't like this at all," I said with a groan.
"There's just too much happening—can I please go home?"
Big Bro said, "If we stay, it'll be okay.
Noises can't hurt you—let's have a good day."

So we stayed, and Big Bro let me chill with his crew.
For lunch, we had my favorite—sweet, smoky barbecue.

Artists showed off paintings, colors gleaming in the sun.
Some of them were about the freedoms Black people had won.

Mom looked my way and gave me a smile,
And I told her it'd be cool if we stayed for a while.

We danced to the BOOM-DIDDY-BEEM of a drum,

And some people sang a song
called "We Shall Overcome."

Speakers **BLARED** loud music

and flags **FLAPPED** in a breeze,

And I grabbed Big Bro's hand and gave it a squeeze.
He helped make this day sweet, like only big brothers could,
And said, "Don't worry, Lil' Bro,

It's all good in the hood!"

Juneteenth was almost over and it started getting dark,
So we said our goodbyes and we left from the park.
I heard a **FLICK-FLICK** coming from the streetlights,
Then I remembered I was scared walking home at night.

What if we get lost?! Was it left? Was it right?
What if we see a stranger looking for a fight?
I'm afraid to see mice or a rat near the trash!
It's very dark out here—"Can we please
    walk fast?!"

Just then, I heard a

RUSTLE RUSTLE

coming from a bush.

Then a **RARR-REOW**,
and I didn't want to look.

RUSTLE RUSTLE

When I heard a loud **HISS**, I was officially scared!
Because I knew for a fact there was a monster in there.

But Big Bro was prepared, no fears about that.
Near the bush, he yelled, "**Boo!**" and out came a cat.

He was smart to think of that, like only big brothers could,
And said, "Don't worry, Lil' Bro, it's all good in the hood!"

We made it back home, but before we went inside
Dad had us sit with him and we looked at the sky.
He said, "Sons, today we celebrated with pride.
We are thankful to be here, to be free, to be alive!"

Just then, dazzling lights began to fly.
Out of nowhere, fireworks brightened up the sky.
They went **FIZZ**, they went **POP**, they went **BOOM**, way up high.
It was awesome, and I couldn't look away if I tried.

Mom came outside with some treats for her boys.
Then Big Bro plugged his ears 'cuz there was a loud noise!
So I leaned over to him, like only lil' brothers could,
And said, "Don't worry, Big Bro!

It's all good in the hood!"

Big sales! Select items only $6.19! About eight years ago, I noticed that Black-owned stores and restaurants in my neighborhood were selling things for six dollars and nineteen cents. I didn't understand why they had picked that price, so I decided to investigate. That's when I learned about Juneteenth, a holiday that is celebrated on June 19 every year. The "6.19" on the price tag was meant to represent that day—a date that would soon become very important to me.

Juneteenth commemorates the end of slavery in the United States. The name is a mix of the words "June" and "19th," which is the date the celebration happens each year. In 1863, during the American Civil War, President Abraham Lincoln signed the Emancipation Proclamation, which was an order that officially freed all the people who were being enslaved in the Confederacy. News of this order spread slowly, as many folks in the Confederate states did not want the enslaved people to be free. But as the Northern troops took over the places that were once held by the Confederacy, the people who had been enslaved in each of those areas were freed. On June 19, 1865, nearly two years after the Emancipation Proclamation was issued, Northern troops took over Galveston, Texas, bringing the news that those previously enslaved people were now free.

I learned about Juneteenth as an adult, but I wish that I had known about it as a kid. Some holidays give me mixed feelings, like I'm an outsider watching others celebrate their stories. But on Juneteenth, I feel free to honor the heritage and legacy of people who look like me. In my neighborhood, we host Juneteenth kick-backs, which are casual parties held in folks' backyards or at local parks. There's always lots of great food and usually music and art, too. It's a day to lift up our culture, our people, our traditions. For Black children like Big Bro and Lil' Bro in this book, it's a day to feel especially proud.

Even though I didn't know about it growing up, Juneteenth is now a cherished holiday for me. If it's 6/19, you can find me somewhere in my hood, celebrating with family, friends, and some tasty food.